THE C

SAWYER CHANTAL: A VAMPIRE WHO WORKS AS AN EMERGENCY MEDICAL TECHNICIAN (EMT.) HIS HOBBY IS PHOTOGRAPHY.

KO MYUNG-SOO, "MUNNY:" AN ADVENTUROUS WEREWOLF WHOSE HOBBY IS GHOST HUNTING.

DELTA CASSIDEY: A PLUCKY MERMAID WHO ALSO IS A GHOST HUNTER AND URBAN EXPLORER.

SAUL GRASSMAN: A SASQUATCH WHO ENJOYS THE HOBBY OF GHOST HUNTING AND OFTEN PARTNERS WITH DELTA TO GO EXPLORING.

THE METRO STATE HOSPITAL (MSH): AN ABANDONED MENTAL HOSPITAL OUTSIDE THE CITY LIMITS OF INNSMOUTH.

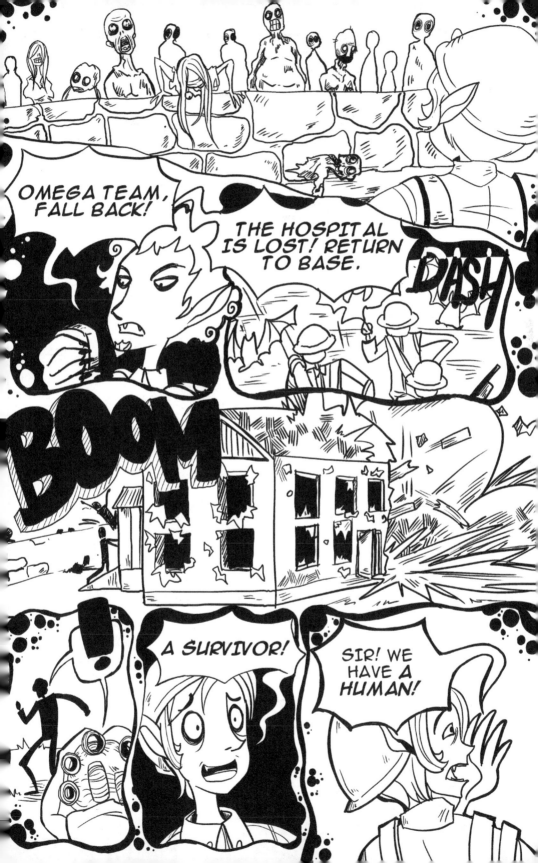

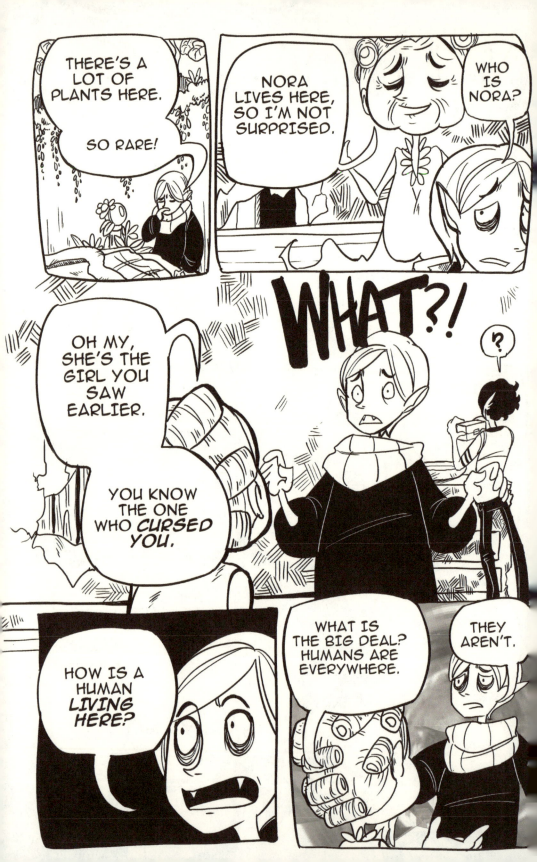

THERE ARE ONLY TWO PLACES WE GHOSTS DON'T GO, THIS FLOOR AND THE *DEATH TUNNEL.*

WHAT DO YOU THINK, GHOST LADY?

HMM?

SKRREEKK

SKREEK

SKREEKK

SKRREEK

RUN BOY!

SOCIAL MEDIA

YOU CAN FOLLOW Klockow Comics & Books through various social media outlets:

 WWW.KATKLOCKOW.COM

 www.webtoons.com/en/

 www.facebook.com/klockowcomics

 @katklockow

 https://tapastic.com/

 http://klockowcomics.deviantart.com

 http://klockowcomics.tumblr.com/

 Instagram @katklockow

ABOUT KAT

Kat is an indie comic book artist and writer and the creator of two graphic novel series. The first is the high-fantasy sereis JINXED, while the other is the horror-fantasy sereis SPIRITUS MAXIMUS.

A paranormal enthusiest and legend tripper, Kat also is the author of two haunted history books, *Haunted Hoosier Halls: Indiana University* and *Ohio's Haunted Crime* with Schiffer Publishing. You can also listen to her host the Paranormal View Radio Show on thePara-X Radio Network and find it on iTunes.